BOOK C ANNOTATED TEACHER'S

MW01688035

We can use the computer!

Rachel Biheller Bunin
and
Maureen Berliner Engeleit

SCHOLASTIC INC.

Senior Vice President, Director of Education: Dr. Ernest Fleishman
Editorial Director: Mickey Revenaugh
Project Director: Sandy Kelley
Vice President, Director, Editorial Design and Production: Will Kefauver
Cover: Type by Glenn Davis; illustrated by Stephen Sweny
Assistant Production Director: Bryan Samolinski

Design and Art Direction: Ned Campbell, Bill SMITH STUDIO
Designer: Christine Sergi, Bill SMITH STUDIO
Illustrators: Bernard Adnet, Stephen Sweny

Acknowledgement: *Oh Calendar* by J. Patrick Lewis.

Printed in the U.S.A.
ISBN 0-590-49550-X
7 8 9 10 3 4 5 6 7 8 9/0

contents

What is a Computer?

A COMPUTER is a machine. When someone says the word *computer,* you may think of a machine that looks like this.

This is a desktop computer. There are many different types of computers. You can find some in your home. Look at the pictures below.

Circle those things that you think have computers in them.

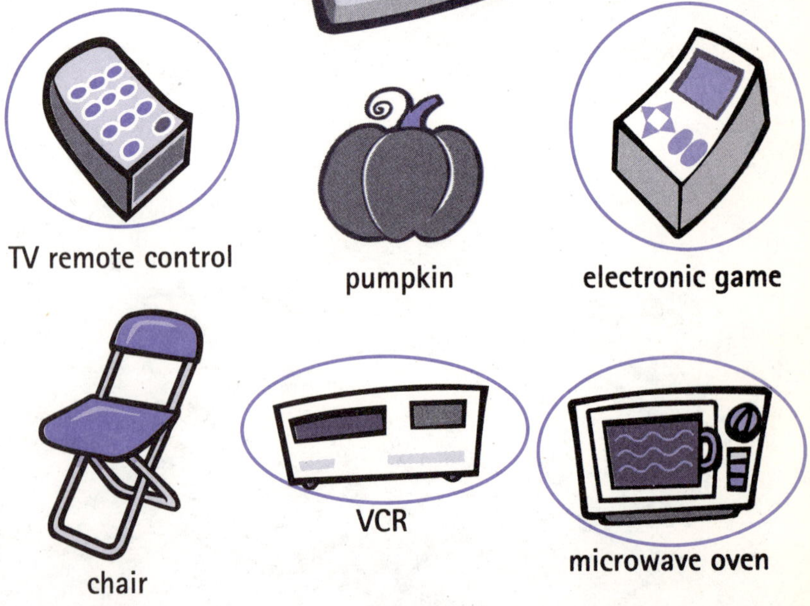

Discuss what all the circled items have in common that makes them "computers."

What Does a Computer Do?

A COMPUTER works with data, or information. Data can be numbers or words or pictures. Here are some examples of data:

Computers all have memory. Computers with a lot of memory can store more numbers, words, or pictures than computers with less memory.

Information that you give a computer is called input. The computer works on, or processes, the input. The CPU is the part of the computer that does the processing.

?

What do you think the letters CPU stand for? Put a check mark ✔ next to the right answer.

- [x] Central Processing Unit
- [ ] Classy Purple Umpire
- [ ] Computer People Users
- [ ] Clear Purple Users

right!

CPU is the central processing unit.

A computer can process information a whole lot faster than you can. It can add lots of numbers quickly. It can let you draw pictures or write stories really quickly.

Besides being fast, a computer doesn't ever get bored. Computers can do things over and over and over again and never get tired or bored.

processing

Put a check mark next to those things that you might find boring or tiring:

- [ ] counting to 10
- [x] counting to 1,000,000
- [ ] writing a letter to your friend
- [x] writing letters to everyone in your school
- [ ] drawing a picture of your mom or dad
- [x] drawing 100 pictures of your mom or dad

When a computer finishes processing the data or input, it gives you **output**.

You may want to save what you have done on your computer. You can store the data on a **floppy disk**.

Discuss how computers can help with these jobs. Why is it better to have a computer do these things?

Input Processing Output

It's really easy to remember the difference between input and output. **Input** goes in. Input is the data you give your computer to work with.

Processing is the process. It is what the computer does to the data. Sometimes processing means adding numbers. Sometimes processing means solving a problem. Computers do all kinds of processing.

Output is what comes out! It is the answer to the problem.

Now let's see if you can figure out the input, processing, and output for these everyday things. Fill in the missing INPUT, PROCESSING, or OUTPUT for each machine.

	machine	input	processing	output
1	VCR	video tape	playing the tape	video picture
2	camera	film	taking pictures	photographs
3	telephone	number	dialing	phone call
4	oven	batter	baking	cake
5	TV remote	channel number	changing channels	new TV show
6	toaster	bread	toasting	toast
7	blender	milk; ice cream	blending	milk shake

Try making up your own:

8	______	______	______	______
9	______	______	______	______

Discuss how data goes into a computer. Ask what kinds of data students would give a computer. What kinds of processing do they think the computer does? What kind of output would they want from the computer?

Hardware

Circle the things that are hard:

WHAT is hardware? Hardware is any part of the computer that you can touch. It is hard, so it is called hardware. If it were wet, you might call it wetware. If it were squishy, you might call it squishyware. But computers are hard. So we call them hardware.

Now let's get back to INPUT for a moment. There is special hardware that lets you get the words, numbers, or pictures into the computer. Somehow you have to be able to tell the computer what you want it to do.

Here are some pictures of the hardware that lets you talk to your computer. Read each description and match it to its picture. Write the correct word under the picture.

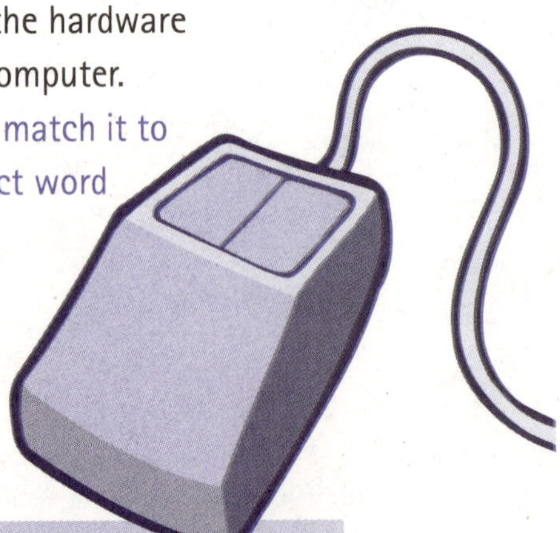

mouse

1 The keyboard has a whole lot of keys on it. These keys are buttons. Each key has a letter or number or symbol or little word on it. By pressing on these keys, you tell the computer what to do. You give the computer input by keying in letters, numbers, or words.

If you have a computer available, point out the hardware components. Find the parts shown on these pages. Name each part and discuss what it does.

2 This is a computer **mouse**. It looks somewhat like a real mouse. It has a short body and a long tail. It may look like a real live mouse, but it doesn't do anything that a real mouse does. A computer mouse lets you give your computer input. To use a mouse, you move it around on a desk or table and click the buttons.

modem

CD-ROM

3 This is a **mouse pen** or **light pen**. It looks like a pen. You can use it like a pen on a special pad. Whatever you write on the special pad will go into the computer.

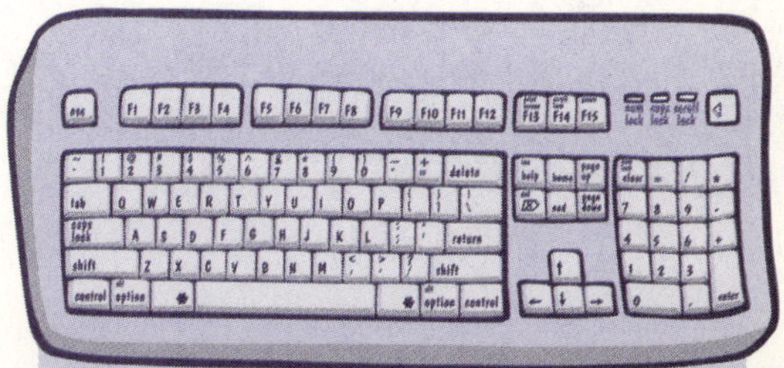

keyboard

4 This is a **modem**. It lets you use your computer to talk to other computers over the telephone lines.

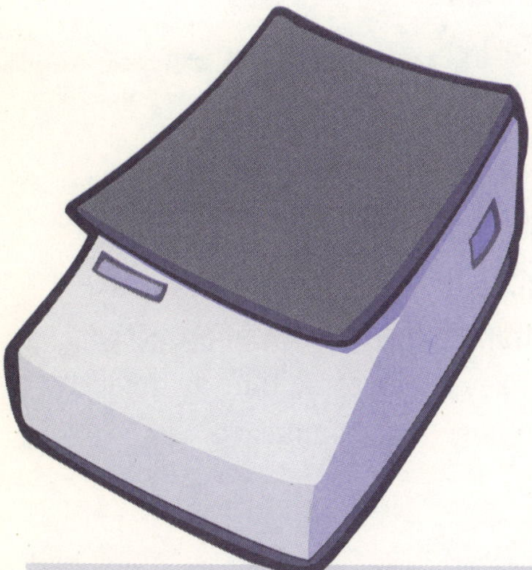

scanner

5 This is a **CD-ROM**. CD-ROM stands for Compact Disk Read-Only Memory. It's a lot like a music CD. It also stores data. In fact, a CD-ROM can store lots of data—much more than the floppy disks. But you cannot store your own data on a CD-ROM.

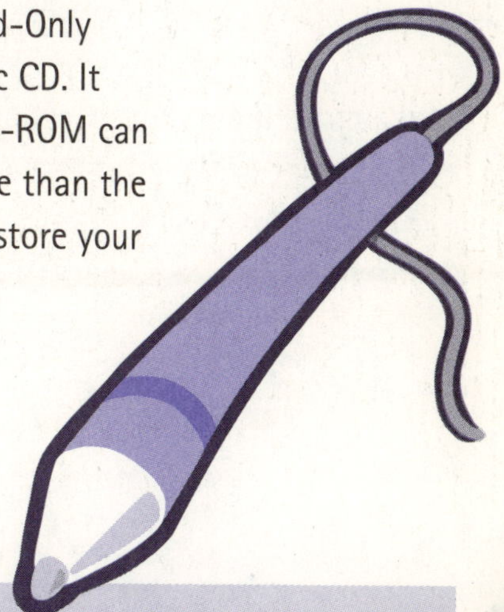

mouse pen

6 This is a **scanner**. It reads the words or pictures or numbers on a page and changes them into a form that a computer can understand.

the Keyboard

THIS is a keyboard. You have to learn keyboarding to key input into your computer. Look at the keyboard. Notice how the letter keys are in the middle divided into three rows.

Write your first name:

____

This is the **shift key**. This key does nothing by itself. You use it to make a capital letter. You have to press the shift key at the same time as the letter you want to be capitalized.

Draw a circle around each key on the keyboard that has a letter that spells your name. Circle each letter once even if your name has the same letter more than once.

Now write your name using all CAPITAL letters:

____

Point out each key on a keyboard in the classroom. Get on-line with a simple word processing program. Have the students press one key at a time to see what it does. Enter a small sample paragraph; then practice using the Shift, Enter, and Escape keys, as well as the Space bar.

You can find the **number keys** on the top row and along the side. You use these keys to input numbers. Draw a big circle around all the number keys.

The long, thin key below the last line of letters is the **space bar**.

What do you think this key does?

It makes spaces.

Right, it makes spaces—spaces between words, spaces between numbers, and just empty spaces!

Find the **Enter key** on the keyboard and circle it.

On some computers, it says **Return**. This key lets you move down a line when you are keying words. It is also the key you press when you want the computer to do something. It is the Do This key. You Enter instructions into the computer with the Enter key.

Shifty types

The shift key has another important job to do. Look at the keys below.

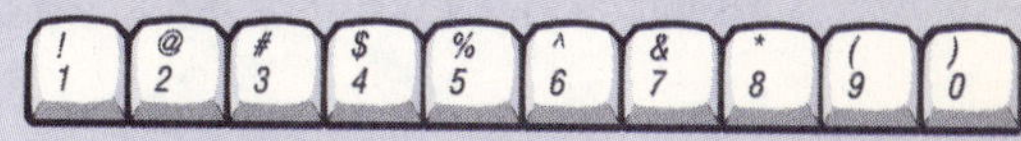

All these keys have two symbols on them. To get the computer to enter the symbol at the top of the key, you have to press the key and the shift key at the same time. For example, if you want to enter an *, you press the *8 key and the shift key at the same time.

For each item below, fill in the symbol that would be entered. The first one has been done for you.

1. Shift + [! 1] ____!____
2. Shift + [@ 2] ____@____
3. Shift + [# 3] ____#____
4. Shift + [$ 4] ____$____
5. Shift + [% 5] ____%____
6. Shift + [^ 6] ____^____
7. Shift + [& 7] ____&____
8. Shift + [* 8] ____*____
9. Shift + [(9] ____(____
10. Shift + [) 0] ____)____
11. Shift + [: ;] ____:____
12. Shift + [" '] ____"____

the Mouse

REMEMBER the mouse? Sort of a cute, furry fellow? No, not really. You learned that the mouse is computer hardware. It is an **input device**. This means the mouse is another way of inputting data into your computer. Do you know how a mouse works?

Be sure that students get plenty of practice pointing, clicking, and dragging the mouse while keeping it on the mouse pad. Pair up two students at each computer. Have one student give directions (up, down, click, left, right, etc.) while the other moves the mouse.

The mouse has a ball underneath it. You push the mouse along a desk or on a pad next to the computer. When you look at your computer screen, you will see an arrow or shape or picture. This is the **cursor**. It tells you where your next letter, number, or symbol will appear. The cursor on the screen will move exactly the same way you move the mouse. This is called **pointing**.

If you turn a mouse over, this is what you'll see.

Find the button on the top of the mouse. Sometimes the mouse you are using will have one button, sometimes two, and sometimes even three! This mouse has one button. This button is really important. It works like the Enter key.

To tell the computer what to do, you first **point** the cursor by moving the mouse. Then when the cursor is just where you want it, you press the button or **click**.

NOW YOU CAN PLAY THE MOUSE GAME

This game will take you through the seasons. First, trace the picture of the mouse on this page. Then cut it out. Put a pencil through the little X. This will be your playing piece.

the Mouse Game

directions:

Find a penny or any coin. For each toss of the coin:

Tails = Point and Heads = Click.

You move the mouse through the maze one square at a time. For each Point (Tails) roll, just move the mouse to the next square. For each Click (Heads) roll, move the mouse and draw a circle around the square you've moved to. At the end of the game, count how many circles you have.

Add up the number of leaves, snowflakes, suns, and flowers you have circled.

☐ snowflakes ☐ suns

☐ leaves ☐ flowers

Which season have you won? ____________

Provide time for students to play the Mouse Game, either alone or in pairs. Be sure they understand the directions for playing. They may enjoy comparing which season they have won.

Monitors and Printers

NOW you know all about input devices. What about getting the data out of the computer? There are two common ways to get your data out. These **output devices** are monitors and printers.

The **monitor** is the screen part of your computer. When you key in letters, you will see them on the monitor. It is like a television screen. That's why sometimes a monitor is called a **screen**. Some computers have color monitors. The output on these screens is in color, just like your color TV. Some computers have screens that can only show output in shades of one color.

You can use a **printer** to have the computer print your output on paper.

Software

REMEMBER when you learned about hardware? That was easy. Hardware is hard. Well, now it's time to learn about **software**. Software is not soft. It is not hard. You can't touch software. Software tells your computer what to do. Software is the programs that run on your computer.

Let's go back to something you already know:

Input → Processing → Output

Software is the processing. It is what makes the computer give you the answer. It is what takes your input and turns it into output. There are two main types of software: **systems software** and **tool software**.

Systems are what make the computer run. It is the system that tells the computer to store your data on a disk. It is the system that gets the program you want to run. The system is like the police officer of the computer.

Find some software. Explain how software is stored on disks—either on a hard disk in the computer or on floppies. Turn on the computer and show how the systems software sets everything up. Discuss different software available in your classroom.

Find some floppy disks that no one needs. Take them apart to show how they are really soft inside. The soft mylar inside is what gives them the name *floppy*.

Tool Software

Tool software does all those boring tasks that were mentioned earlier. There are many types of tool software that you can use on your computer. The type of software you need depends on the job you want to do.

draw a line to match the tool to the picture.

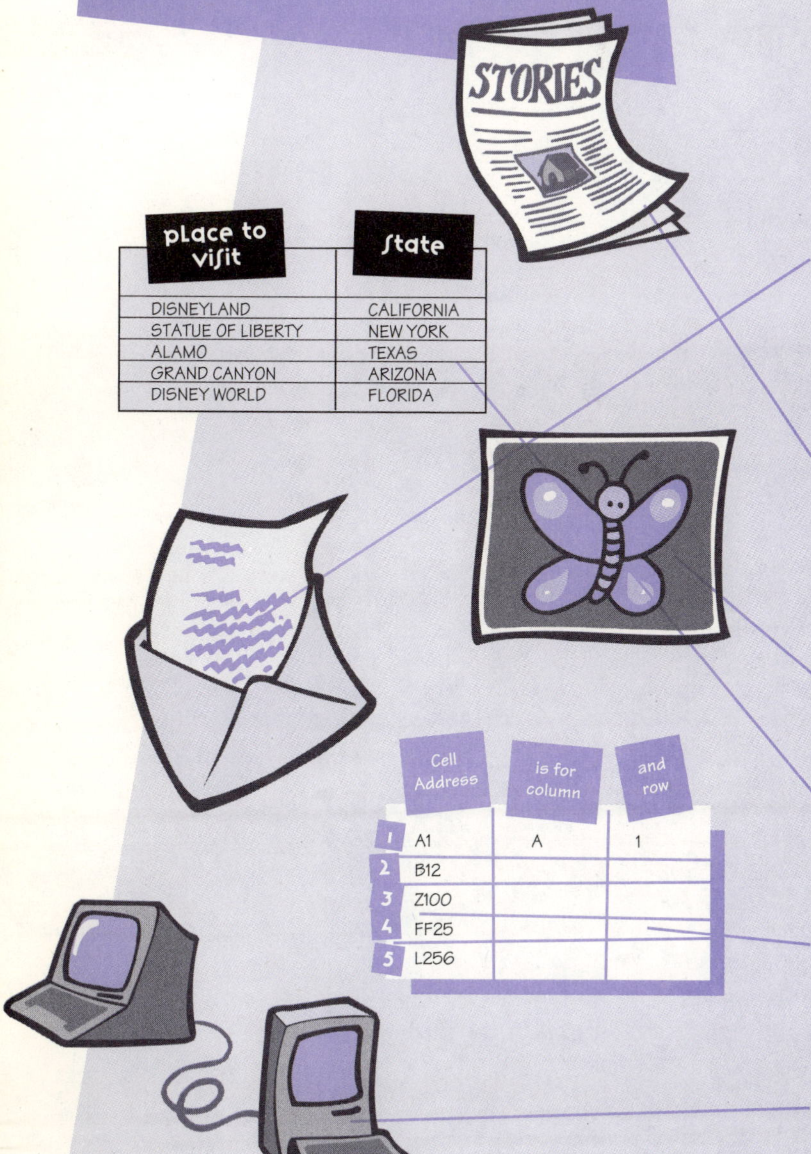

Word processing software works with words to help you write letters, notes, or anything that you can write with pen and paper.

Desktop publishing software takes the words that you write and places them on pages with pictures and fancy lettering. You can publish newsletters, newspapers, or even books by using this tool.

Graphics software lets you create art on your computer.

Database software helps you to organize and keep track of lists of information.

Spreadsheet software helps you add, subtract, multiply, and divide numbers.

Communications software helps you talk to your computer, lets your computer talk to other computers, and lets you talk with other computers.

Discuss possible uses for each type of software in the classroom. How can the different software tools help students with math, reading and writing, science, and social studies?

Graphical User Interfaces: GUIs

HOW do you tell your computer what to do? You use Graphical User Interfaces, or GUIs. That's hard to pronounce. You can call them "gooeys". GUIs use pictures or graphics to help you tell your computer what to do. These pictures are called **icons**. You use the mouse to point and click on the icons. The icon looks like what you want to do.

Here's an example. If you saw an icon that looked like this:

What do you think it would do?

____

____

____

Right! It would tell the computer to **PRINT** whatever you were working on.

Let's see if you can match the icon to what it does.

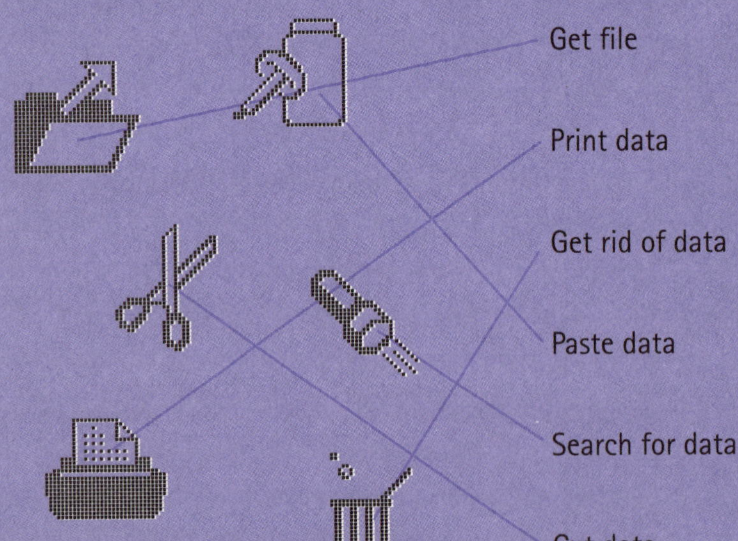

Go on-line with a GUI interface. Have students determine which icons do what. Display a pull-down menu and explain how each of the items below each main option is a suboption. This is a good way to practice mouse techniques.

Complete the Puzzle!

Across

2. Computer screens
5. The data that goes in
7. The data that comes out
8. Software and ______
10. It lets your computer talk to another computer

Down

1. A machine to store and process data
3. To make a capital letter, press the ______ key.
4. The "do this" key
6. It gives you output on paper
9. CD ______

What is Word Processing?

WORD PROCESSING is more than just keyboarding. With word processing software, you can key a story as fast as you can. You will learn how to move letters, words, paragraphs, and pages with the touch of a key. When you keyboard, your words appear on a monitor, not on a piece of paper. When you are finished working on your story, you print it out.

There are special words you need to know in order to do word processing. First of all, the letters, numbers, and special signs that you see on the keyboard are called characters. Characters make up the words, or text, of what you key.

The computer doesn't care whether you are writing a report for school or a letter to your pen pal across the world. What you are keying is called a document. When you are keying the document for the first time, you say you are *creating a document*. Does that sound confusing to you? If it does, don't worry. You will be meeting these words again.

Circle the activities you think you could do with word processing.

1. Write a poem about the merry month of May.
2. Decorate your classroom with snowflakes for the month of January.
3. Add a sentence to a ghost story you made up.
4. Correct a word that you spelled incorrectly.
5. Fly a kite.
6. Do your math homework.
7. Tell your friend how to bake a cake.
8. Write a recipe to send to your friend.
9. Send the recipe to hundreds of friends and family members.

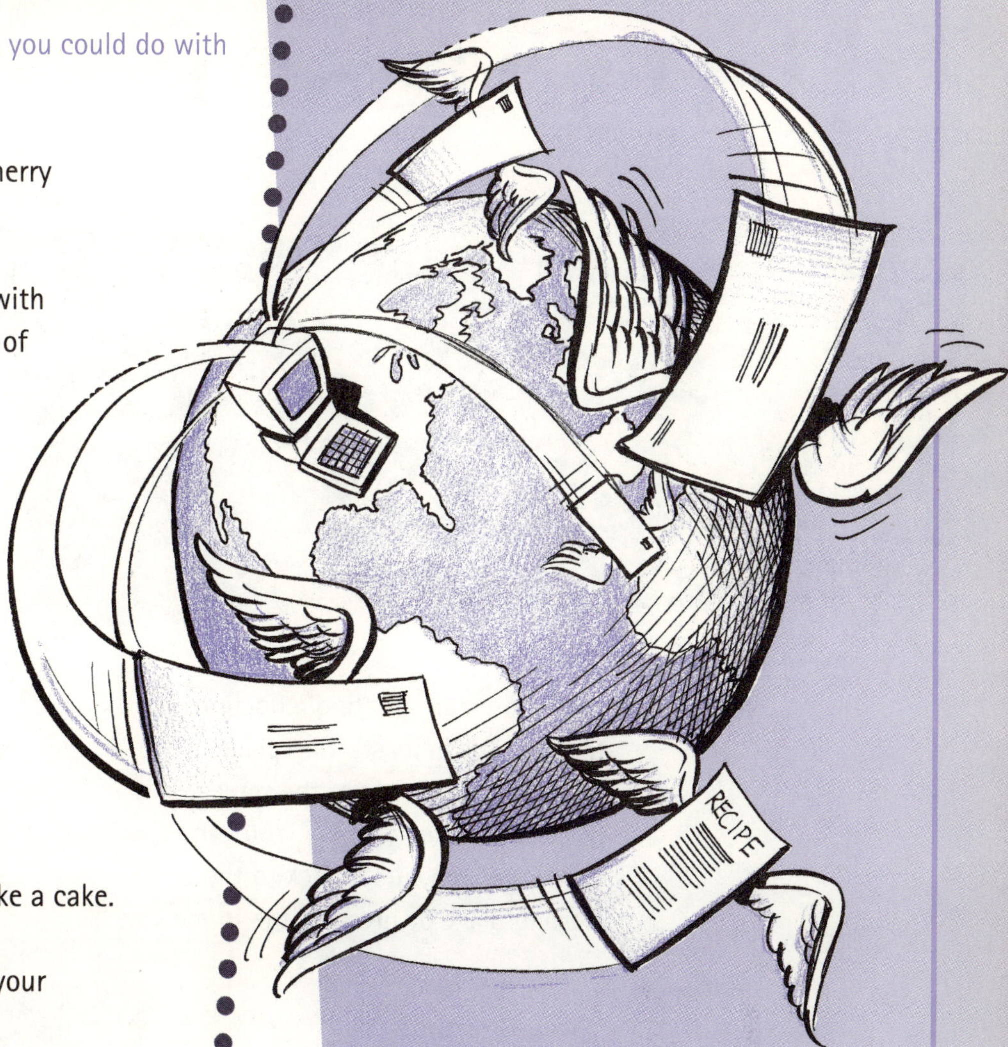

Discuss other tasks that can be done with word processing.

The Cursor

THE cursor is very important to word processing. It is a place holder. It lets you know where you are. In some software the cursor is a blinking line. In others it is a lighted block.

When you start creating a document, the cursor is in its starting place in the top left-hand corner of the screen. This position is called Home. You can always get the cursor back to the starting place by pressing the Home key.

You move the cursor around by using the arrow keys or the mouse.

The cursor is the square around the "O" in the title of the poem on the opposite page. Follow the directions below and place a square around the character the cursor would be on.

1. Press the ↓ 2 times.
2. Press the → 4 times.
3. Press the ↓ 4 times.
4. Press the ↓ 3 times.
5. Press the → 7 times.

Oh Calendar

To see
December press
Its face against the door,
I realize I've grown an inch
Or more
Since we
First hung you up.
You measured time by turns:
Hard winter nights to softball days,
Sunburns,
The chill
At Halloween,
Then! rumors of reindeer
Across the sky. Goodbye, Happy
Old Year!

—J. Patrick Lewis

Enter the poem into your word processing program. Follow the directions to move the cursor on-line.

Spaces and Tabs

DID you ever wonder why the space bar is the largest key on the keyboard? Well, the space bar just might be the most used key on the keyboard. If there was no space bar, this sentence would look like this:

Iftherewasnospacebar,thissentencewouldlooklikethis.

Now, draw a line where each space should go.

NOW that you understand about the space bar, it's time to learn about the Tab key. The Tab key lets you move the cursor more than one space at a time. When you create a document, you decide how many spaces make up one tab.

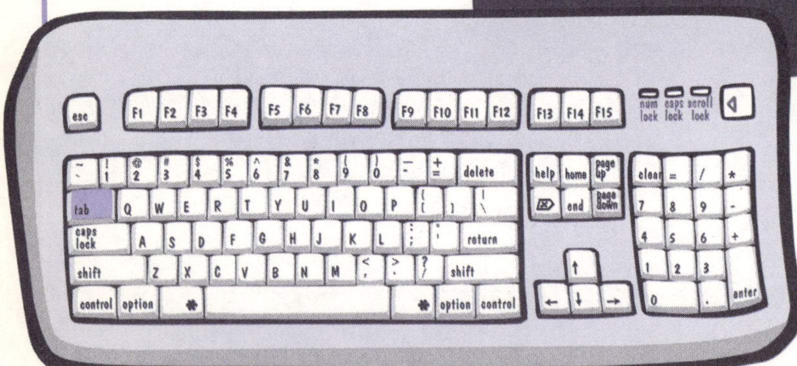

the tab game

1. Get twenty index cards.
2. Label four of each of the cards with "1," four with "2," four with "3," four with "4," and four with "TAB."
3. Shuffle them and put them face down.
4. Trace a playing piece from the top of page 25 and cut out your tracing.

HOW TO PLAY!

You need two people. The youngest person goes first. Pick a card. If you pick a number card, move that number of spaces. If you pick a TAB card, jump 5 spaces. The first person to get to DECEMBER 31 wins.

***Good* Luck!**

the players
Jim
Maria
Ron
Susan
HAPPY NEW YEAR
the tab game
start
winter
summer
end
DEC. 31st
fall
spring

Fonts and Points

ONE of the really cool things that you can do with word processing is to change the style of the letters you use. **STOP NOW!** That got your attention, didn't it? These different styles of type are called **fonts**. Font styles have names.

Now you make a font to match the mood of each word below the line.

____________	____________	____________	____________
Angry	Scared	Silly	Happy

A **point** is a measurement of how big the font will be. The larger the number, the bigger your letters will be. The larger the characters are, the fewer of them will fit on a line.

Below is a word shown in different point sizes. Under each size is a ruler.
Count how many characters fit into an inch.

1. SNOWFLAKE — 6 characters fit into an inch
2. SNOWFLAKE — 4 characters fit into an inch
3. SNOWFLAKE — 8 characters fit into an inch

Type the word SNOWFLAKE several times on-line and change to different fonts and point sizes to show students the differences.

Editing a Document

deleting text

Sometimes your finger will hit a wrong key. To correct the mistake, you must take away, or **delete**, the character. To do this, you can press the arrow keys in the direction of the mistake until the cursor reaches the character to be deleted. If you have a mouse, point to the character you want deleted and click. When the cursor is in the correct position, press the **Delete** key. The character disappears, and the other characters rush in to fill its space. The sentence below has a mistake. The square—the cursor—is in the right position to delete the incorrect character.

April showers bring May floewers.

Now press the Delete key. This is how your sentence would look:

April showers bring May flowers.

NOW you are ready to print, but OOOPS! You see a word that is misspelled. And wait—wouldn't that sentence be better at the end of the paragraph? It seems that you have some editing work ahead of you.

Now it is your turn. Put a square around the letter that should be deleted in each sentence.

1. Each year there are four seatsons — spring, summer, fall, and winter.
2. The springstime party will be at the park.
3. Snowflakes wiull decorate the classroom at the winter party.
4. Bobtbing for apples will be a great game to play at the fall party.
5. We can eat shot dogs and lemonade at the summer party.
6. At the summer party we can decorate the schoolyard with seashtells, beachballs, and sand.
7. Hot chocolate and marshmallows will be the food to eat at the winster party.

Copy the sentences into the word processing program and do the editing on-line. As spelling practice, have students work in pairs, one creating a sentence with a spelling error and the other correcting it.

Inserting Text

WHEN you deleted a character, the remaining text on the line moved closer together. Now you want to add, or **insert**, text. Instead of coming closer together, the old characters make room for the new characters by moving down in the line.

Inserting text is just as simple as deleting it. You move your cursor, by using the arrows or by pointing and clicking with the mouse, to the place on the line where you need to insert the text. Then you key it in. Watch all the other characters move over.

Here is a Valentine's Day rebus. On each picture in the poem, write the word that should be inserted. Choose from the word box. Place the cursor, a square, around the first character to be inserted.

rebus valentine

You may not carrot all for me

The way I care for you.

You may turnip your nose

When I plead with you —

But if your heart should beet with mine

Forever lettuce hope

There is no reason in the world

Why we two cantaloupe .

Word box

carrot
turnip
beet
lettuce
cantaloupe

Have students write a paragraph about their favorite season, leaving out some words. Have another student edit the paragraph, inserting the missing words.

Cutting and Pasting Text

YOU have a problem. A whole paragraph from your document has to be moved to the end of the text. How do you get it there without deleting and re-keying the text? Word processing is a very powerful tool. You can solve this problem with two simple commands. The first command is called **cutting**, and the other is called **pasting**. Here's how you do it.

1. Move the cursor to the first character you want to cut.

   beachball I went to the seashore with my.

2. Highlight the whole word with the cursor

   beachball I went to the seashore with my.

3. Press the Cut command key. This is what you will see now.

   I went to the seashore with my.

4. Move the cursor to the place where you want the word to be placed.

   I went to the seashore with my .

5. Press the Paste command key.

   I went to the seashore with my beachball.

This might seem like a lot of work for just one word, but think how little work it is when you want to move paragraphs, or even pages!

Have students write their own riddles and mix up the answers below. Have them exchange papers with another student, who cuts and pastes the answers in the right place.

Here are some riddles about the seasons. Under the riddles are all the answers. Cut out each answer and paste it by the riddle.

riddles

1. What did the cloud have under its raincoat?

   Answer: Thunderwear

2. What do witches study in school?

   Answer: Spelling

3. Where do bedbugs get married?

   Answer: In the spring

4. What president liked to do his laundry?

   Answer: George Washing-ton

5. What did the hot dog say when he crossed the finish line?

   Answer: I'm the wiener.

6. How do bees go to school?

   Answer: In the buzz

answers

George Washing - ton	Spelling	I'm the wiener.
In the buzz	Thunderwear	In the spring

Saving a Document

NOW you want to save your document. To save a document you must give it a name. Your document is going to be a file on your disk. Do you think you should name it Tanya or Michael? No! Give your documents names that tell what the document is about.

File names should also be short. When you are writing lists for a fall party, you might want to give your document a name like "FALLIST."

Here are short descriptions of some documents. Circle the file name you think is best.

1. A poem about the calendar

   NOSE   CALEND   END YEAR

2. A shopping list for the winter party

   WINLIST   ICY   COAT

3. A list of students in your class

   HOUSE   CLASLIST   FEET

4. A poem about Thanksgiving Day

   ELECTION   MEMDAY   THANKS

5. A list of decorations for the spring party

   DECORATE   DWEEB   DRINKS

Have students write a brief poem about their favorite holiday and save the file with a meaningful name.

Printing a Document

YOU have done everything you were supposed to do with your document. But not once, in all this time, have you seen your document printed out on a sheet of paper. When do you think that happens? Well, now, of course!

All computers have a **print command**, but not all computers have printers hooked up to them.

Before you print your document, you must be sure your computer has a printer. When you are sure, press the print command key. The computer will ask you which file or document is to be printed. You enter the file name and press Enter.

Remember the documents you named on the last page? Here is a description of each document. Write the file name in the blank space, so that it can be printed.

1. A poem about the calendar PRINT FILE: CALEND
2. A shopping list for a winter party PRINT FILE: WINLIST
3. A list of students in your class PRINT FILE: CLASLIST
4. A poem about Thanksgiving Day PRINT FILE: THANKS
5. A list of decorations for the spring party PRINT FILE: DECORATE

Have students print out their files.

Name It!

Word List

Tab	fonts
characters	cursor
Home	inserting
file name	creating
pasting	deleting

Fill in each blank with the correct word from the list above

1. Letters, numbers, and special signs that are on the keyboard are called ___characters___.
2. The ___cursor___ is a place holder that lets you know where you are.
3. When you type a document for the first time, you say you are ___creating___ a document.
4. You can always bring the cursor to the top left-hand corner of your screen by pressing the ___Home___ key.
5. The ___Tab___ key lets you move the cursor more than one space at a time.
6. Different styles of type are called ___fonts___.
7. When you erase characters or text, you are ___deleting___ them.
8. When you add characters or text, you are ___inserting___ them.
9. Moving text from one area to another in your document is called cutting and ___pasting___.
10. When you save a document, you give it a ___file name___.

For additional on-line practice, have students try writing a short report on why leaves change color in the fall or what makes the seasons change, and then have them key it in with a word processing program.

What is

Desktop Publishing

DESKTOP PUBLISHING software is used to make most of the printed materials that you see every day. It is used to make newspapers and magazines. When you see words and pictures, or text and graphics, together on a printed page, it is likely that desktop publishing was used to design and make it.

Just 20 years ago, it took hundreds of people to help publish a newspaper. People trained for years to become typesetters, printers, and inkers.

Put a check mark next to the item if you think that desktop publishing was used to make it.

- [ ] The pattern on the new fall dress your mother is wearing
- [x] The program for the ice show you went to see last winter
- [x] A menu from the restaurant where your family ate during summer vacation
- [ ] The words cut into the watch your brother got for graduation

Find examples of desktop publishing around your classroom, for example, on your bulletin boards. Point out the graphics, headlines, and text.

Terms You Need to Know

THERE are many words that are used in desktop publishing. You are going to learn about four of the most important ones.

See the large words at the top of the page? Those words have a special name because they appear at the head of the page. Can you think of their special name? You're right! They are called **headlines**. Headlines appear at the top of a page or the beginning of a story or article. You want to design your headline to be eye-catching. That is what makes people want to read it and the story underneath. In some desktop publishing software, headlines have different names, but they are all the same thing.

Next are the words that tell your story. These words are **text**. You have already worked with text in word processing. Do you remember that by using different fonts and points you can make your text more interesting?

Do you see the picture above? There are lots of pictures in this book. Pictures are called **graphics**. Graphics can be anything that is not words. There are many kinds of graphics. There are graphs and pictures that you draw. **Clip art** is a collection of pictures that someone else drew that you can find on disks. The graphic to the right is an example of clip art.

Name Your Terms

Name each example below by writing H for headline, T for text, or G for graphic in the box

April showers bring
May flowers.

T

SKIER
WINS RACE

H

SCHOOL
OPENS

H

G

School ends on June 28.
What are you doing over the summer vacation?

T

EXTRA!
READ ALL
ABOUT IT!!

H

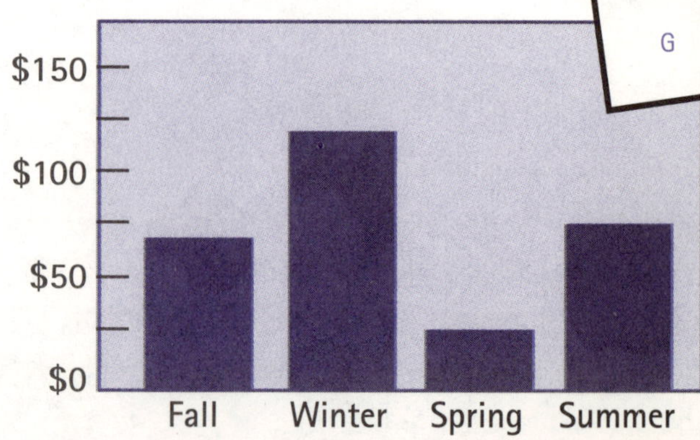

G

Designing a Seasonal Newsletter

NOW that you have learned about headlines, text, and graphics, you can begin to design your seasonal newsletter. Designing means laying out the page. You will not be writing the stories or choosing the graphics now. You will decide where on the page they will be placed.

to start

Get a blank sheet of 8 1/2-by-11-inch paper. This will be your newsletter page.

Your newsletter will have these things:

1. One big headline giving the name of your newsletter
2. Two smaller headlines to title your stories
3. Two text stories. Lay them out one after the other.
4. Two graphics, one for each story

On a blank sheet of paper trace the shapes labeled headlines, graphics, and stories on the next page. Cut out the pieces and paste them on the blank page you are using for your design layout.

Follow the instructions on-line to design a newsletter about the current season, using a desktop publishing program.

Name of your Newsletter

Headline 1

Headline 2

graphic 1

graphic 2

story number one

story number two

Writing a Seasonal Newsletter

NOW you have to fill in the actual headlines, stories, and graphics that you are going to put into your newsletter.

Let's start with the headline that will be the name of your newsletter. Have you decided on a name yet? Write some ideas in the space below.

____

____

____

Now decide which name you like best. Put a star next to it. Then copy your title headline in the space at the top of your layout page.

What will your stories be about? You might want to write about the holidays coming up. How about a story about people whose birthdays will be this season? Write some of your story ideas on the lines below.

____

____

____

When you decide what your stories will be, write them in the spaces provided on your layout page.

With the stories written, you can now think of a title for each one. Try out some story titles on the lines below.

____

____

____

____

Put stars next to the titles you like best. Then write them in the spaces provided on your layout page.

Graphics for Your Newsletter

YOU have written the headlines and text. All that is left is to pick out the graphics that you will use. In one graphic space you will use a picture that you draw. In the other graphic space you will use clip art.

If your story was about Presidents' Day, you might look in magazines for pictures of cherry trees or log cabins. Write two picture ideas for each story below.

Clip art is a collection of graphics—photographs, diagrams, maps, and drawings by other people—that you can find in books or on disks. The graphics can be cut out and put into whatever you publish. Your job now is to look in magazines and find pictures that will make your newsletter more interesting and exciting.

remember

The pictures that you use must fit into the graphic space you have allowed for them on your layout page.

1. The first snowstorm of winter. **Picture ideas:**

   ____

   ____

2. The color of the changing leaves in fall.
   Picture ideas:

   ____

   ____

3. Ways to cool off in the heat of the summer.
   Picture ideas:

   ____

   ____

Have several magazines available for students to browse through for picture ideas.

Now you need some of your own artwork for the newsletter. You can create your own art right on the computer. When you create artwork on the computer, you won't get paint on yourself or the floor. If you create something that you don't like, you can easily erase it or move things around.

Here is a picture that you can color in now.

Drawings on the computer are made up of hundreds of dots called **pixels**. It is like a color-by-number drawing card.

1	1	1	1	1	1	1	1	1	1	1	1	1	1	1	1	1	1	1	1	1	1	1	1	1	1	1	1	1	1	1	1	1	1	1	1
1	1	2	2	2	1	1	1	1	1	1	1	1	1	1	1	1	1	1	1	1	1	1	1	1	1	1	1	1	1	1	2	2	2	1	1
1	2	2	2	2	2	2	2	2	1	1	1	1	1	1	1	1	1	1	1	1	1	1	1	1	1	1	2	2	2	2	2	2	2	2	1
1	2	2	2	2	2	2	2	2	2	2	2	1	1	1	1	1	1	1	1	1	1	1	1	2	2	2	2	2	2	2	2	2	2	2	1
1	2	2	2	3	3	3	3	2	2	2	2	2	2	1	1	1	1	1	1	1	1	2	2	2	2	2	2	3	3	3	3	2	2	2	1
1	1	2	2	3	3	3	3	3	3	3	2	2	2	2	1	1	1	1	1	1	2	2	2	2	3	3	3	3	3	3	3	2	2	1	1
1	1	2	2	2	3	3	3	3	3	3	3	3	2	2	2	1	2	2	1	2	2	2	3	3	3	3	3	3	3	3	2	2	2	1	1
1	1	1	2	2	3	3	4	4	4	3	3	3	3	2	2	2	2	2	2	2	2	3	3	3	3	4	4	4	3	3	2	2	1	1	1
1	1	1	2	2	3	3	3	4	4	4	4	3	3	3	2	2	2	2	2	2	3	3	3	4	4	4	4	3	3	3	2	2	1	1	1
1	1	1	2	2	2	3	3	4	4	4	4	4	3	3	3	3	2	2	3	3	3	3	4	4	4	4	4	3	3	2	2	2	1	1	1
1	1	1	1	2	2	3	3	4	4	4	4	4	4	3	3	3	2	2	3	3	3	4	4	4	4	4	4	3	3	2	2	1	1	1	1
1	1	1	1	2	2	3	3	3	4	4	5	5	4	4	3	3	2	2	3	3	4	4	5	5	4	4	3	3	3	2	2	1	1	1	1
1	1	1	1	2	2	2	3	3	4	4	5	5	4	4	4	3	2	2	3	4	4	4	5	5	4	4	3	3	2	2	2	1	1	1	1
1	1	1	1	1	2	2	3	3	3	4	4	4	4	4	3	3	2	2	3	3	4	4	4	4	4	3	3	3	2	2	1	1	1	1	1
1	1	1	1	1	2	2	3	3	3	3	4	4	4	4	3	3	2	2	3	3	4	4	4	4	3	3	3	3	2	2	1	1	1	1	1
1	1	1	1	1	2	2	2	3	3	3	3	3	4	3	3	3	2	2	3	3	3	4	3	3	3	3	3	2	2	2	1	1	1	1	1
1	1	1	1	1	1	2	2	2	2	3	3	3	3	3	3	3	2	2	3	3	3	3	3	3	3	2	2	2	2	1	1	1	1	1	1
1	1	1	1	1	1	1	2	2	2	2	2	3	3	3	3	3	2	2	3	3	3	3	3	2	2	2	2	2	1	1	1	1	1	1	1
1	1	1	1	1	1	1	1	1	2	2	2	2	3	3	3	3	2	2	3	3	3	3	2	2	2	2	1	1	1	1	1	1	1	1	1
1	1	1	1	1	1	1	1	1	1	1	2	2	3	3	2	2	2	2	2	2	3	3	2	2	1	1	1	1	1	1	1	1	1	1	1
1	1	1	1	1	1	1	1	1	2	2	2	2	3	2	2	2	2	2	2	2	2	3	2	2	2	1	1	1	1	1	1	1	1	1	1
1	1	1	1	1	1	1	1	2	2	2	2	3	2	2	2	1	2	2	1	2	2	2	3	2	2	2	2	1	1	1	1	1	1	1	1
1	1	1	1	1	1	1	1	2	2	3	3	3	2	2	2	1	2	2	1	2	2	2	3	3	3	2	2	1	1	1	1	1	1	1	1
1	1	1	1	1	1	1	1	2	2	5	3	2	2	2	1	1	2	2	1	1	2	2	2	3	5	2	2	1	1	1	1	1	1	1	1
1	1	1	1	1	1	1	2	2	2	2	2	2	2	2	1	1	1	1	1	1	2	2	2	2	2	2	2	2	1	1	1	1	1	1	1
1	1	1	1	1	1	2	2	2	2	2	2	2	1	1	1	1	1	1	1	1	1	1	2	2	2	2	2	2	2	1	1	1	1	1	1
1	1	1	1	1	2	2	2	2	1	1	1	1	1	1	1	1	1	1	1	1	1	1	1	1	1	1	2	2	2	2	1	1	1	1	1
1	1	1	1	1	1	1	1	1	1	1	1	1	1	1	1	1	1	1	1	1	1	1	1	1	1	1	1	1	1	1	1	1	1	1	1

1 blue
2 purple
3 red
4 Light green
5 dark green

Drawing Tools

ARTISTS use all kinds of tools. They might pour a bucket of paint over a canvas or use spray paint. Artists use thick or thin brushes for different kinds of strokes. These tools and more are yours when you create art on a computer. The tools show up on the screen in little pictures called **icons**. You use the mouse to select and use a tool.

Here is a list of drawing icons and what they do:

fills the screen with a color you choose. You can usually select a pattern as well.

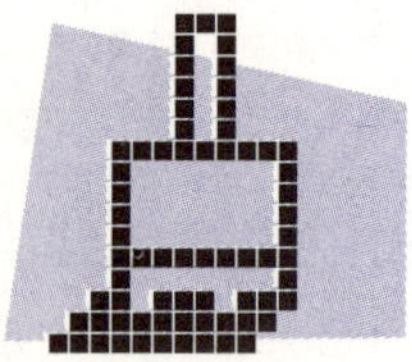

lets you make different types of brush strokes.

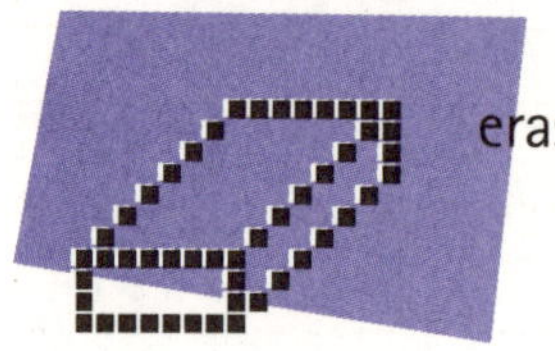

erases part of a picture.

lets you make perfect squares.

lets you make perfect circles.

lets you draw straight lines.

Get on-line with a graphics or desktop publishing program. Have students experiment with the different drawing tools to create pictures.

draw a Line

Draw a line to match the picture to the drawing tool that was used.

Now that you know about all the drawing tools that you can use, you can draw a picture for your newsletter. Remember, you have to draw a picture the right size to fit into your layout. Good drawing!!

Resizing

IF YOU have outgrown your favorite jeans, wouldn't it be nice if you could make them bigger so that you could wear them again? You could **resize** them. Well, that is just what you do in desktop publishing. If a story you have written is too large for the space you laid out, you can make that space larger. If the picture you want to put in the newsletter is too big, you can make it smaller. Resizing doesn't delete or insert anything into the graphics or the text. Resizing lets you make your text and graphics fit into your design layout.

Look at this group of pictures. Some pictures are the same, but have been resized.

Have students pull a text box, headline, or graphic into a document and use the resizing tool to see how it changes.

Word Find

Find these words about desktop publishing in the puzzle below. The words may go up or down or across. Some words are backwards. When you find each word, circle it.

TEXT HEADLINE
GRAPHIC CLIP ART
RESIZE ICON PIXEL

find

A	Y	X	T	B	C	F	K	D	G	V	H
C	U	L	E	M	S	N	Q	B	P	C	R
Z	S	D	X	O	E	T	F	K	G	N	Z
C	H	X	T	W	J	V	H	U	L	O	M
L	N	R	Q	P	B	Z	E	Y	C	C	D
I	E	V	F	T	G	R	A	P	H	I	C
P	A	Z	B	Y	C	X	D	W	F	E	V
A	U	H	J	T	I	K	L	R	L	Q	P
R	K	Z	Y	L	E	X	I	P	D	U	P
T	H	S	E	Q	G	I	N	J	N	R	O
A	Z	R	E	S	I	Z	E	M	O	D	W
F	S	T	P	E	Z	O	A	Y	B	K	M

If students have enjoyed creating a seasonal newsletter, they might wish to continue it for other seasons, or even to make it a monthly publication to be shared within the class or among other classes.

What is a Database?

DATA is information. A database is a collection of information about things. It is important to organize your things or your data so that you can use them. If everything you own was in one big box, it would be very hard to find what you need when you need it.

How do you store and organize your things? Draw lines to match each thing to all the places you could keep it.

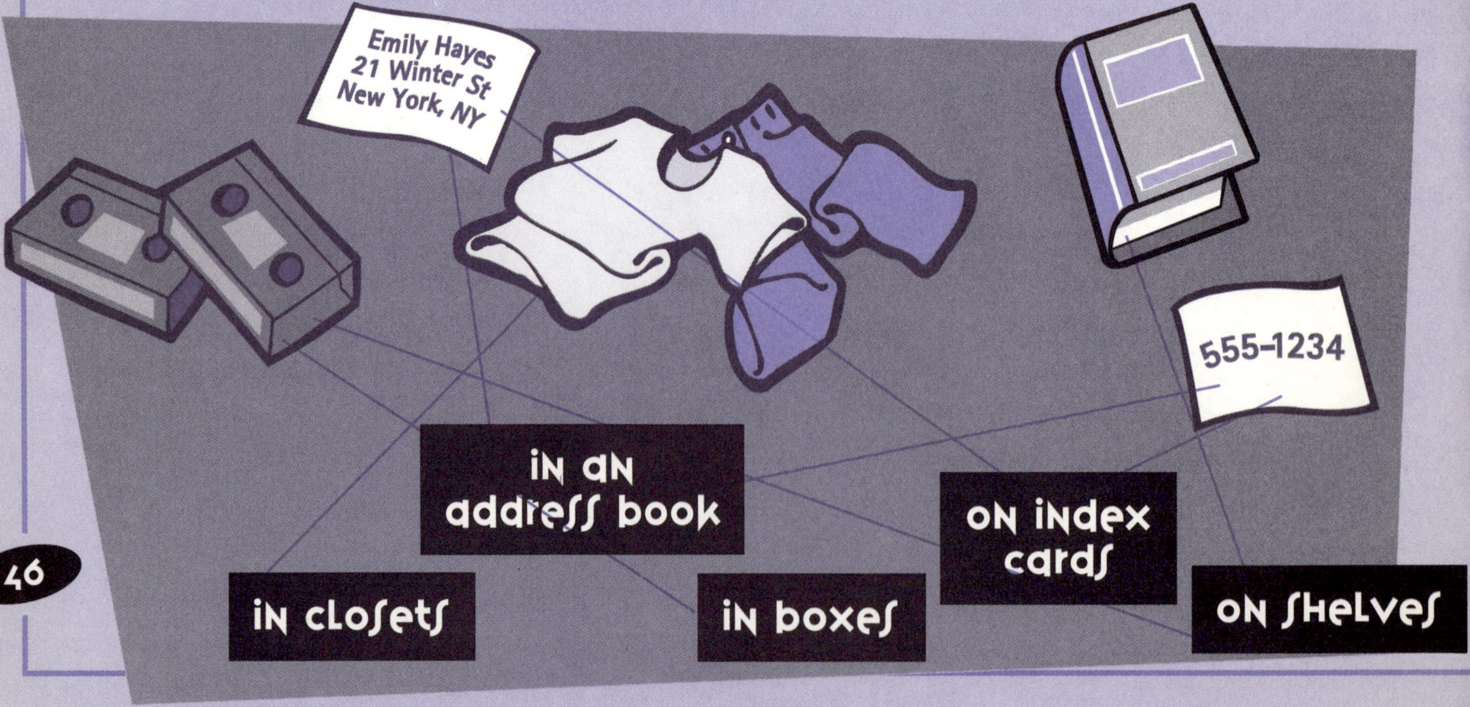

Database software is a computer tool that you can use to organize and store your data.

Which lists do you keep? Put a check mark next to each one.

- ☐ Names, addresses, and phone numbers of your friends
- ☐ Titles of books you have read
- ☐ Birthday presents you received
- ☐ Computer games that you play or own
- ☐ Toys you own
- ☐ Food to serve at a party
- ☐ Items to buy at the supermarket

Can you think of other lists you keep?

____

____

A **field** is an item of information.

A **record** is a collection of fields that have something in common.

A **file** is a collection of records that have something in common.

You will learn all about fields, records, and files as you create your own database to plan parties throughout the year.

Many different people use databases in their work. Look at the workers listed below. Write what kind of information might be in their databases.

video store owners

lists of the titles of tapes they own;

lists of who has rented tapes

Librarians

lists of titles and authors of books;

lists of which books have been loaned out

doctors

lists of names and addresses of patients;

lists of diseases and symptoms

telephone operators

lists of names, phone numbers, and addresses

chefs

lists of recipes they like to cook;

lists of ingredients they keep in the pantry

teachers

lists of the children in their class;

lists of grades

Students may wish to discuss ways that parents or other relatives use databases in their jobs.

Using Fields to Plan a Party

LET'S plan some parties during different seasons of the year. At the beginning of October, will you give out apple cider? During the months of January and February will you decorate the classroom with paper snowflakes?

Planning several parties could be confusing, but the database will help you. Let's create a database file to help you plan. The file name will be Parties. No two field names can be the same. But that's no problem. The field names will be: MONTH, SEASON, DRINK, MUSIC, and DECORATIONS.

Draw lines to connect each MONTH field to the SEASON, DRINK, MUSIC, and DECORATIONS fields that describe it.

Month	Season	Drink	Music	Decorations
July	Winter	Hot chocolate	Let it Snow	Snowflakes
September	Spring	Lemonade	Take Me Out to the Ballgame	Baseball cards
January	Summer	Lemonade	By the Sea	Seashells
March	Fall	Apple cider	Falling Leaves	Colored leaves

Now that all the fields are connected, you have created four records. Each row is a record.

Adding Records to the File

You want the database to include the games that you will play at the parties. Add a GAME field to your file.

Now you are ready to add some data. Enter the data for each month in the correct box. You can have the same data in more than one record.

month	season	drink	game
january	winter	hot chocolate	
february	winter		
march	spring		
april	spring		
may	spring		
june	summer		
july	summer	lemonade	
august	summer		
september	fall	apple cider	
october	fall		
november	fall		
december	winter		

Have students compare and discuss their choices of drinks and games for each month.

Records in a File

LABEL a manila file folder "PARTIES." This is your file. There are four Party Record Cards below. Each record has seven fields. Fill in the missing data for each field. Can you make the eight record cards for the months that are missing? Use a separate index card or piece of paper for each month. Remember to use the same field names. This will be your database file.

party

MONTH: July
SEASON: Summer
DRINK: Lemonade
FOOD: Pizza
DECORATIONS: Seashells
GAME: ______
MUSIC: ______

party

MONTH: January
SEASON: Winter
DRINK: Hot Chocolate
FOOD: ______
DECORATIONS: Snowflakes
GAME: ______
MUSIC: ______

Now you have 12 records in your parties file. Next, you will be learning how to sort your data

party

MONTH: March
SEASON: Spring
DRINK: Lemonade
FOOD: ______
DECORATIONS: Baseball Cards
GAME: ______
MUSIC: ______

party

MONTH: September
SEASON: Fall
DRINK: Apple Cider
FOOD: ______
DECORATIONS: Colored Leaves
GAME: ______
MUSIC: ______

Get on-line and create a file called PARTIES. Set up the record and field sizes. Let students take turns entering the data from their record cards.

Sorting a Database File

SORTING a database file is as easy as ABC or ZYX. When you put words in A,B,C order, that is called **ascending alphabetical order**. When you put words in Z, Y, X order, that is called **descending alphabetical order**.

Let's practice sorting words. Put the words listed below in ascending alphabetical order.

A b c d e f g H i j k L M
N o p q r s t u v w x y z

season	blossom
flowers	flowers
ice	ice
wading	season
blossom	wading

Now put the words listed below in descending alphabetical order.

z y x w v u t s r q p o N
M L k j i H g f e d c b A

planting	weeding
weeding	sow
harvest	reap
sow	planting
reap	harvest

Now that you understand about sorting, let's sort your PARTIES file. Pick a record and sort the fields in that record in ascending alphabetical order. You can do it!

Have children line up in alphabetical order to sort by the alphabet. Then line them up in size order to sort by sizes. On-line have them sort the PARTIES file by different fields. Let them see if the computer is faster than a person. Divide into two teams. One team will work at the computer, and the other team will work on the hard copy. Sort fields in ascending and descending order.

Queries

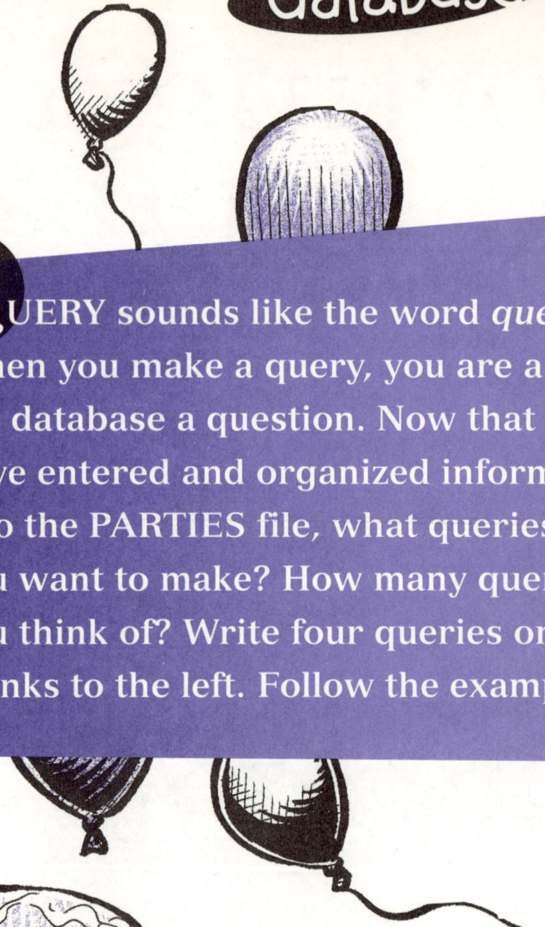

QUERY sounds like the word *question*. When you make a query, you are asking the database a question. Now that you have entered and organized information into the PARTIES file, what queries would you want to make? How many queries can you think of? Write four queries on the blanks to the left. Follow the example.

queries

What decorations will we use in the month of June?

____

____

____

____

Using your PARTIES database, answer the following queries.

1. How many records have the same food?

____

2. What is the drink that will be served at the March party?

____

3. At how many parties is the same game going to be played?

____

Remember, this file has only 12 records. It is small. Think how useful queries are if your file has more than 100 records.

Use a TV-guide grid as an example of a database. Discuss different types of queries students might have; for example, how many shows are about horses this week? Or, is the actor Luke Perry on more than one show this week? Have students create queries for their database. Who can find the answers faster—the computer or a person? Get into teams again.

True or False

read each sentence. decide whether the sentence is true or false, and circle your answer.

1. Information is data. True False
2. A field is a collection of records that have something in common. True False
3. A file is a collection of records that have something in common. True False
4. Database software is a computer tool that helps you write letters. True False
5. You cannot have the same data in more than one record. True False
6. The field name should give you an idea of the kind of information to be entered in the field. True False
7. Field names are often the same. True False
8. These words are in ascending alphabetical order: cat, house, jacket, lollipop. True False
9. A query is like a question. True False
10. A database program cannot answer queries. True False

What is a Spreadsheet?

A **SPREADSHEET** is a computer software program. It is a computer tool. With a spreadsheet you can add, subtract, multiply, and divide numbers. You can make **graphs** to see your numbers as pictures.

The number 5 by itself doesn't mean much. But if you are trying to figure out how many bottles of cider to buy for the fall party, 5 *bottles* is **data.** The added information turns numbers into data. Circle the numbers that are data:

25 kids

cider costs $1.50

20 snowflakes in the window

156

Spreadsheets are very useful for working out budgets. A **budget** helps you plan how much money you need to buy things.

party List

Put a check mark next to those things that could be part of your budget spreadsheet. Remember, a spreadsheet only works with numbers.

- [x] the cost of a bottle of cider
- [x] the price of popcorn
- [ ] the color of the leaf decorations
- [x] the number of kids in the class
- [x] the amount of money each kid put in the party box

Can you think of other data you might need for your party budget?

____

____

Discuss the concept of a budget. Begin to plan the budget for a party for an upcoming seasonal celebration in your class. Discuss all the items that might be appropriate for the budget.

How is a computer spreadsheet program different from a calculator? When you use a calculator to add, subtract, multiply, or divide, you have to key in each number every time.

When you use a spreadsheet, you enter all the data once. If one or two numbers change, you only have to enter the new numbers to find the answers.

Let's plan to have a party to celebrate each season! You cannot spend more than you have. But maybe the cost of watermelon for the summer party is less than the cost of apples for the fall party. Use the money saved in the summer to pay for the apples in the fall. The PARTY SPREADSHEET will help you figure this out.

Here is how the spreadsheet for all four parties would look:

	A	B	C	D	E
1	SEASON	$ collected	cost of drinks	cost of food	total costs for parties
2	Fall	$50	$10	$17	$27
3	Winter	$50	$20	$30	$50
4	Spring	$25	$5	$8	$13
5	Summer	$25	$10	$20	$30
6	TOTAL	$150.00	$45.00	$75.00	$120.00

The spreadsheet has already done some work by figuring out the total costs for each party. Fill in the totals on the blank lines.

Use your spreadsheet to answer these questions:

1. Which is the most expensive party? the winter party
2. Which party has the most expensive food? the winter party
3. Which is the cheapest party? the spring party
4. How much money have you collected for the year? $150.00
5. Do you have enough money to pay for all the parties? yes

the Worksheet

A SPREADSHEET program uses a worksheet to organize data.

The worksheet is made up of **rows** and **columns**. Rows go across, like this:

Draw another row here:

Columns go up and down like this:

Draw two more columns next to the one above.

Be sure that the students understand the concept that worksheets organize data in rows and columns. You may wish to bring in an accountants' paper worksheet and explain that the spreadsheet is an electronic representation of the paper worksheet.

When the rows and columns are laid upon each other, a **grid** is formed. This is a tic-tac-toe game board. It has a grid of 3 columns and 3 rows.

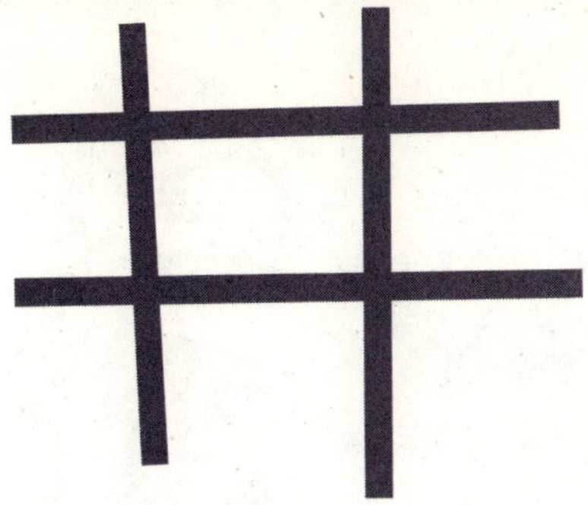

Each box that is formed when a row crosses a column is called a **cell**. Draw a grid that has 4 rows and 4 columns below.

1	2	3	4
5	6	7	8
9	10	11	12
13	14	15	16

You can put numbers or words into **cells**. Starting with the number 1 and going across, put one number in each cell of the grid that you just drew.

What was the last number you put in the grid?.............................. 16

As you can see, a grid with 4 rows and 4 columns gives you a worksheet with 16 cells.

Here is another worksheet with 4 columns and 4 rows. Each column has a letter at the top. The first column is column A. The second column is column B.

Each row has its own number on the left side of the worksheet. The numbers go down in order. The first row is row 1, the second row is row 2. Complete the column letters and row numbers for this worksheet.

	A	B	C	D
1	Soda	.75	4	$3.00
2	Corn	1.00	5	$5.00
3	Snack	1.50	5	$7.50
4	Total	3.25		$15.50

Cell Addresses

YOU just learned that columns are lettered and rows are numbered. Each cell in the worksheet has a **cell address**.

What is your address?

____

____

Split it up into its parts. Does it have a number? Write it here

Are there letters for the street name? Write them here.

The cell address is made up of the column letter and row number put together. Cell addresses look like this: **A5, B6, C16, F39.** Depending on the spreadsheet program, you can have so many rows and columns that a cell address might even look like this: **ZZ100.**

When you are working with spreadsheets, you will use the cell address to find the data you need. Let's practice. The first one is done for you.

	cell address:	is for column:	and row:
1	A5	A	5
2	C45	C	45
3	D37	D	37
4	GG2	GG	2
5	A27	A	27

If students live on a numbered street, tell them to use the street number in the street name box, or have them spell out the numbers. Go on-line with a spreadsheet and locate various cell addresses. Have students play games finding entries in cells using cell addresses.

Now use cell addresses to decode secret words. The grid contains all the letters of the alphabet and the numbers 1-10. Find each letter by using its cell address, and write each secret word. The first one is done for you.

	a	b	c	d	e	f
1	A	B	C	D	E	F
2	G	H	I	J	K	L
3	M	N	O	P	Q	R
4	S	T	U	V	W	X
5	Y	Z	1	2	3	4
6	5	6	7	8	9	10

secret words

1. F1 F2 A1 A2 FLAG
2. A4 E4 C2 A3 SWIM
3. A4 B3 C3 E4 SNOW
4. A4 F2 E1 D1 SLED
5. C1 C2 D1 E1 F3 CIDER
6. F1 F2 C3 E4 E1 F3 FLOWER
7. D3 C4 A3 D3 E2 C2 B3 PUMPKIN
8. D3 C3 C3 F2 POOL

Have the students think of other seasonal words and make up secret codes for further practice with cell addresses.

Labels and Values

WHEN you plan the budget for your parties, you will need to put numbers and words in the cells in your worksheet. Remember when you learned about numbers and data? If you just have the number 5 in a cell, you won't know if it means 5 dollars, 5 classmates, or 5 cider bottles.

In spreadsheets, words are called labels. When you put numbers in cells, they are called values. The labels tell you what the values mean. Here is a list. Put the letter V next to all the values. Put the letter L next to all the labels.

L winter	V 15	L one	L pumpkin
L party	V 7	V 25,000	

Let's take another look at the budget worksheet for your parties.

	A	B	C	D	E
1	SEASON	$ collected	cost of drinks	cost of food	total costs for parties
2	Fall	$50	$10	$17	$27
3	Winter	$50	$20	$30	$50
4	Spring	$25	$5	$8	$13
5	Summer	$25	$10	$20	$30
6	TOTAL	$150	$45	$75	$120

There are 10 cells that have labels in them. Can you find them? Write their cell addresses here:

A1	A6
A2	B1
A3	C1
A4	D1
A5	E1

In spreadsheets, values are used for computations. Labels are descriptive. Enter values and labels into a spreadsheet. Be sure to show how some numbers can be labels, such as phone numbers or social security numbers.

Formulas

In math, formulas can go across or down. Fill in the answers.

3 + 1= 4

6 - 2= 4

2 x 6= 12

2)4= 2

3	4	6
X6	+5	-5
18	9	1

SPREADSHEETS allow you to ask "WHAT IF?" What if you collected $35 for each party? If you had to figure out how much money you would have left after each party and then for the year, it would be a lot of work. With the spreadsheet, all you have to do is change the numbers in column B and the formulas will figure out all the new totals.

Spreadsheets use symbols called computer notation. The symbols are on these keys on the keyboard:

For addition use a +.

For subtraction use a -.

For multiplication use an *.

For division use a /.

Did you notice that the computer notation for addition and subtraction is the same as when you write math formulas yourself? The computer notation for multiplication and division is different. In the empty box, write the computer notation for each formula.

1. 5 + 6= 11   +
2. 3 - 2= 1   -
3. 5 x 2= 10   *
4. 6 ÷ 2= 3   /

Spreadsheets can use formulas to add, subtract, multiply, or divide the values in cells. But spreadsheets don't always use numbers, they use cell addresses. Spreadsheet formulas look like this. Draw a line to connect each formula to the type of math it does.

A1 + B1= C1	division
A1 - B1= C1	multiplication
A1/B1= C1	addition
A1*B1= C1	subtraction

Load a spreadsheet program into your computer and create a file called PARTIES for the budgets discussed in this lesson. You and the students should be able to enter all the numbers and formulas.

Adding a Column

Formulas in spreadsheets can have many cell addresses. Use this simple spreadsheet to fill in the answers for the following formulas. The first one is done for you.

	A	B	C
1	4	5	6
2	3	2	1

1. A1 + B1 * C1 = [4] + [5] + [6] = [15]
2. C1 – C2 = 6 - 1 = 5
3. C1/B2 = 6/2 = 3
4. B2 * A2 * A1 = 2*3*4 = 24

As you can see, you can use a spreadsheet to figure out all kinds of things. You may want to figure out how much supplies for decorating your classroom will cost for each season, each month, or each major holiday. It all depends on what you want to know about the data.

Here is your budget worksheet again. Do you see anything that looks different? Instead of numbers, some cells have formulas. The formulas figured out the totals. Two formulas are missing. Here they are. Your job is to put each in the right cell.

D2 + D3 + D4 + D5   C5 + D5

	A	B	C	D	E
1	SEASON	$ collected	cost of drinks	cost of food	total costs
2	Fall	$50	$10	$17	C2+D2
3	Winter	$50	$20	$30	C3+D3
4	Spring	$25	$5	$8	C4+D4
5	Summer	$25	$10	$20	C5 + D5
6	TOTAL	$B2+B3+B4+B5	C2+C3+C4+C5	D2 + D3 + D4 + D5	E2+E3+E4+E5

It is important for students to understand that the formulas in spreadsheets allow you to change the value in one cell to see how it affects the other cells. Enter the spreadsheet for the Party budget. Change some values in the cells to show how formulas compute values. Formulas tell the spreadsheet to use values in different cells to "find the answer."

Data as Pictures: Graphing

SPREADSHEET software can create charts and graphs to let you see your data as pictures. Spreadsheets can create pie charts, bar graphs, and line graphs. Pie charts make your data look like pies, bar graphs make your data look like bars, and line graphs show your data as lines.

Here are two ways of showing you how much your parties cost. Each season's total is graphed. The tallest bar tells you which party costs the most. The biggest slice of pie tells you which party costs the most. The winter party costs the most.

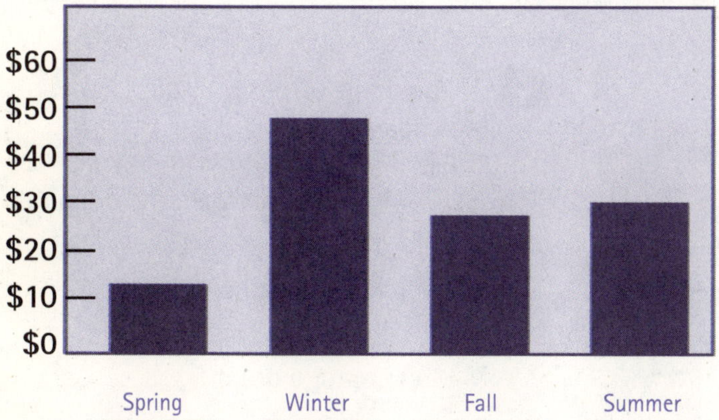

Write the word Winter on the biggest slice and on the tallest bar.

Go back to the spreadsheet on page 60 and look at the totals. Fill in the correct labels for each bar and each slice of pie.

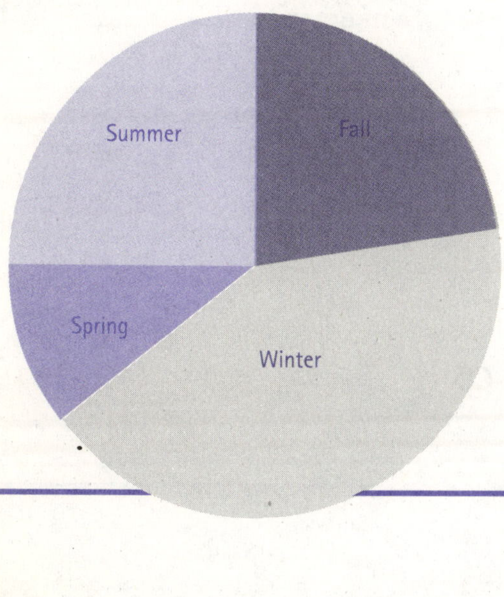

Create a bar graph and a pie graph from the party spreadsheet on-line.

Fill in the Box

1 A computer software tool that helps add, subtract, and multiply numbers is called a .... [b]

a] bedspread
b] spreadsheet
c] database
d] calculator

2 Spreadsheet software uses [b] to organize the data.

a] windows
b] worksheets
c] cars

3 The worksheet is made up of rows and

columns
____

4 The words in a spreadsheet are called [a]

a] labels
b] text
c] values
d] words

5 In a worksheet, cell addresses are made up of the column letter and row [a]

a] number
b] address
c] letter
d] value

6 In a worksheet, if you wanted to add two numbers together you would enter a [c] into a cell.

a] value
b] label
c] formula
d] word

7 The symbol for multiplication in a spreadsheet is....................... [*]

8 The symbol for division in a spreadsheet is.............................. [/]

9 If you want to see your data as a picture, you can.................. [c]

a] buy a camera and take a photo of your worksheet
b] get a pencil and paper and draw a picture of your data
c] create a graph

10 Which of these is NOT a kind of graph?....................................... [d]

a] pie
b] bar
c] line
d] bubble

Have each student take a turn creating a budget for one seasonal party. They should list all the items they would have to purchase, entering each item as a label in column A. Enter the price per item in column B. Enter the number of items needed in column C. Use a multiplication formula to figure out the total costs in column D.